The Fox and the Stork

Based on a story by Aesop

Retold by
Mairi Mackinnon

Illustrated by
Rocío Martínez

Reading Consultant: Alison Kelly
Roehampton University

Fox and Stork
were friends,

2

but Fox loved
playing tricks.

3

One day, he
had an idea.

He asked Stork
to dinner.

5

Stork was very hungry.

Fox poured soup
into wide bowls.

9

Poor Stork!

She couldn't eat a thing.

11

The next day, Stork
asked Fox to dinner.

16

Stork poured soup
into tall jars.

Poor Fox! He couldn't eat a thing.

Fox was angry.
"You tricked me!"

But Stork said,
"You tricked me first."

21

"Always be kind to your friends," said Stork,

"and they
will be kind
to you."

23

Puzzles

Puzzle 1

Help Fox spot the differences.
There are eight to find.

Puzzle 2
How is Stork
feeling?
Match each
sentence to
a picture.

I'm not sorry.
I'm annoyed.
I'm hungry.
I'm excited.

C

D

27

Puzzle 3
Choose the best sentence in each picture.

A

28

C

I can't eat!

I can't wait!

D

It's your fault.

It's your turn.

Answers to puzzles

Puzzle 1

Puzzle 2

 I'm excited.

A

I'm hungry.

B

 I'm annoyed.

C

I'm not sorry.

D

Puzzle 3

A

"Is it ready?"

C

"I can't wait!"

B

"What's the matter?"

D

"It's your fault."

About the story

The Fox and the Stork is one of Aesop's Fables, a collection of stories first told in Ancient Greece around 4,000 years ago. The stories always have a "moral" (a message or lesson) at the end.

Series editor: Lesley Sims

Designed by Non Figg

First published in 2007 by Usborne Publishing Ltd., Usborne House,
83-85 Saffron Hill, London EC1N 8RT, England. www.usborne.com
Copyright © 2007 Usborne Publishing Ltd.